VICTORY ★ SCHOOL SUPERSTARS

WITHDRAWN

Sports Illustrated KIDS

STONE ARCH BOOKS
a capstone imprint

I Just Have to Ride the Halfpipe!

by Jessica Gunderson
illustrated by Jorge Santillan

STONE ARCH BOOKS
a capstone imprint

VICTORY SCHOOL SUPERSTARS

Sports Illustrated KIDS *I Just Have to Ride The Halfpipe!*
is published by Stone Arch Books — A Capstone Imprint
151 Good Counsel Drive, P.O. Box 669
Mankato, Minnesota 56002
www.capstonepub.com

Art Director: Bob Lentz
Graphic Designer: Hilary Wacholz
Production Specialist: Michelle Biedscheid

Timeline photo credits: Shutterstock/Pavel Mikushin (top left);
Sports Illustrated/Al Tielemans (bottom left), Robert Beck, (middle
& bottom right); Wikipedia, (top right).

Printed in the United States of America in Stevens Point, Wisconsin.
032011   006111WZF11

Library of Congress Cataloging-in-Publication Data
Gunderson, Jessica.
I just have to ride the halfpipe / by Jessica Gunderson ; illustrated by
Jorge H. Santillan.
    p. cm. — (Sports Illustrated kids. Victory School superstars)
Summary: Kenzie uses her super strength skill to learn snowboarding
ISBN 978-1-4342-2236-7 (library binding)
ISBN 978-1-4342-3397-4 (pbk.)
    1. Snowboarding—Juvenile fiction. 2. Friendship—Juvenile fiction.
[1. Snowboarding—Fiction. 2. Friendship—Fiction.] I. Santillan, Jorge,
ill. II. Title. III. Series: Sports Illustrated kids. Victory School superstars.
    PZ7.G963Iak 2011
    [Fic]—dc22   2011002307

TABLE of CONTENTS

KENZIE WINZ

Snowboarding

AGE: 10
GRADE: 4
SUPER SPORTS ABILITY: Super strength

Triumph Mountain
Superstars:

 KENZIE ALICIA DANNY

TRIUMPH MOUNTAIN

Triumph Mountain is the leading sports-education resort in the country. It is home to dozens of ski lifts and a state-of-the-art ice arena and snowboard park. At Triumph, young athletes can learn their favorite winter sports from their favorite athletes.

1. Ice Arena
2. Lodge
3. Condos
4. Halfpipe
5. Jumps
6. Ski Slopes

Triumph Mountain

"I'm so excited to ski!" Carmen says. "I love trying new sports. Don't you?"

"I guess," I say with a sigh.

I am not too excited about the skis on my feet or the poles in my hands. But at least the view from the top of this small slope is nice.

I'm on a school trip to Triumph
Mountain. For weeks, everyone has been
excited to ski. But not me. I'd rather be
back in our school gym doing backflips.

Other kids from Victory School are
already gliding down the slopes, cheering
and laughing. So far, no one has fallen.

But I'm sure I will within minutes.

"What if I fall?" I ask Carmen. "I'm not going to be any good."

"Don't worry about being good. Just have fun!" she says.

"But I like being good. And I'm good at gymnastics, nothing else," I say.

"Of course you are," Carmen argues. "Who else can bench press a picnic table?"

I laugh. "No one else at Victory," I agree.

Victory School is a place for outstanding athletes. Each of us has a special skill.

Carmen, for example, has a perfect dribble. The basketball moves from her hand to the floor and back to her hand like magic.

My skill is super strength. I'm stronger
than anyone I know, even my dad! My
strength has helped me in gymnastics, but
I often struggle to keep it under control.

"Here I go!" Carmen says, and she glides
down the hill.

I'm the last one left. I wobble to the edge of the slope. My feet feel heavy and awkward. I'm used to being a graceful gymnast. Now I'm a clumsy bundle of nerves with sticks strapped to my feet.

I push off gently, hoping for the best. But as I start to slide, my feet turn in different directions. My skis crash together, and I fall on my behind.

I hope no one was watching.

But I know there is no hope when I hear a girl's voice behind me. "First time at Triumph?" she asks.

Gymnastics in the Snow

I glare up at the girl. She's grinning, which only makes me glare harder. "What makes you say that?" I growl.

"Oh, don't be mad," she says cheerfully.

I try to stand, but my skis slide and I fall again.

"I'm Zoey," the girl says, reaching down to help me up. "I don't like skiing either," she whispers with a grin.

"These winter sports aren't my thing," I agree. "I usually stay inside when it snows."

Zoey nods. "I'd never even seen snow until I came here," she says. "I'm from Hawaii."

"Wow!" I say. I haven't met many people from other places. We Victory kids tend to stick together. "Do you play any sports there?" I ask.

"I'm a surfer," Zoey says.

"I'm no better at water sports than I am at winter sports," I admit.

Remembering my misadventures in the pool earlier this year makes me cringe. I hated swimming because I wasn't good at it. Once, I got so angry I kicked the diving board, and it fell into the pool.

"Gymnastics is my sport," I tell her.

Zoey's eyes brighten. "I know the perfect winter sport for you!"

"You do?" I look at her doubtfully. "It had better be indoors."

"No, silly. Follow me," Zoey says. "You are going to love this!"

I follow Zoey to Triumph Mountain's snowboard park, a giant, snowy area with ramps of all sizes and long rails. A halfpipe is carved in the center. It is a long, U-shaped ramp with a flat part in the middle.

"I'm not sure if snowboarding is going to be any better than skiing," I start to complain. Then I stop and stare.

Snowboarders zoom from one side of the halfpipe to the other, catching air off the lip. One makes a half turn in the air before coming back down.

Another grabs the side of her snowboard while airborne. Next to the pipe, a snowboarder leaps onto a rail and slides across it, landing upright and taking off again.

I can't believe what I am seeing. "It's like gymnastics in the snow!" I say. I tug Zoey's arm and head toward the halfpipe. "Let's go! I just *have* to ride the halfpipe!"

Beginner's Slope

"Not so fast. The beginner's slope is this way," Zoey says, tugging me in the opposite direction. "There are a few things you have to learn before you can try out the park."

"Like what?" I ask.

"Like did you know that riding goofy doesn't mean you're silly? It means you're riding with your right foot in front,"she says.

I follow her to the beginner's slope, even though I'd rather try the park first. Zoey introduces me to José, a member of the Olympic snowboarding team.

"I'm a gymnast," I tell him.

José smiles at me. "So you must have great balance," he says.

"I used to have a hard time on the balance beam," I tell him. "Once I even broke a beam in front a huge crowd of people. But I'm good at it now."

"Balance, flexibility, and control are skills you need for snowboarding," José tells me.

He shows me how to sideslip down the slope by keeping the board horizontal. Then he shows me how to ride regular.

"The most important thing is to get used to the board," he says.

I fall a few times, but soon I'm sliding easily. I'm surprised by how natural the board feels. Soon, I'm doing small jumps called ollies.

"You catch on fast," José says. "Ready to try some tricks at the park?"

"I thought you'd never ask!" I say.

CHAPTER 4

Cartwheels in the Sky

Even though I'm excited, I'm a little nervous to ride the rails. I zoom toward a small, short rail. "It's no higher than the balance beam," I tell myself.

I use my strength to ollie onto the rail, fly across it, land on the other side, and carve to a stop. Snow flies from the back of my board like a white rainbow.

"Next stop, halfpipe!" I say when I meet up with José and Zoey.

"Are you sure you're ready?" José asks.

"You bet," I say. "I'm a gymnast. I'm comfortable flying in the air!"

I drop into the halfpipe, taking it slow and easy until I'm used to the feel of the pipe. Then I speed up.

When I reach the lip, I push off with all my strength. Well, okay, not *all* my strength. That would've sent me to the moon!

But I do fly high into the air. The park turns upside-down as I flip head over heels. It's like a cartwheel in the sky.

I could do this all day, but I need a break. I zoom toward Zoey and José. They are watching me, amazed.

"You were right," I tell Zoey. "I think snowboarding is the perfect winter sport for me."

"I knew it," she says. "A gymnast and a surfer. We're quite the snowboarding pair!"

Avalanche!

I'm laughing with Zoey when I hear it. A low grumbling that sounds like it's coming from the belly of the mountain.

I grip Zoey's arm.

"What's that noise?" she asks.

"Avalanche?" I whisper, my throat caught with fear.

Zoey shakes her head, looking over my shoulder at the rim of the hill. "It's no avalanche," she says, pointing.

I turn slowly, afraid to look. I squint against the glare of the sun on the snow.

Then I see them. It's the Victory kids, trudging toward the snowboarding park.

"Who are they?" asks Zoey.

"The Victory School Superstars," I say.
I realize why they are making so much
noise. They aren't just walking. They're
stomping angrily. And groaning and
muttering.

"I guess they don't want to snowboard," Zoey says.

"I guess not," I reply with a laugh.

We follow the Victory kids to the beginner's slope. They're as bad on snowboards as I am on skis.

Josh falls backward as soon as he straps the board to his feet. The twins, Kim and Tim, slide and fall at the same time.

"Falling is part of learning," José tells them over their grumbles.

"You'll get the hang of it in no time," Zoey adds.

I watch, bored, as the Victory kids go up and down the slope, falling over and over.

"Come on, Zoey. Let's take a break and head in for a snack," I say finally.

"Don't you want to help your friends?" Zoey asks. She points toward Josh, who has fallen in the snow.

I suppose she's right, but I'm too tired. I trudge toward the lodge. I'm ready for some hot cocoa.

Then I see someone in the shadows of the trees.

It's Carmen. And she doesn't look happy.

Snow Dribbling

"Carmen! Why aren't you snowboarding with the others?" I ask.

She shrugs. She's pounding a snowball together with her hands. Then she lets it fall from her palm to the ground. She stares at it like she's waiting for it to bounce back up.

"Carmen," I say, "are you trying to dribble? With a snowball?"

She shrugs again. "It's the only thing I'm good at."

"That's not true!" I say. "Besides, remember what you told me earlier? You said not to worry about being good."

"I guess I did say that," she admits.

"And you know what? Your advice really helped me. Especially with snowboarding. I tried it, and I had a lot of fun!" I say.

"Well, I tried too. And I just keep falling," she says.

"Falling is part of learning," I tell her, remembering what José said. "Come on. Give it one more try. I'll help you."

Carmen tosses another snowball to the ground. "All right," she says.

I remember some of the things José and Zoey told me. "Keep your front knee flexed and your back leg relaxed," I tell Carmen at the top of the slope. "Turn your head and body in the direction you want to go."

Carmen makes it to the bottom of the beginner's slope without falling once. At the bottom of the hill, she turns and gives me a thumbs-up.

I do a thumbs-up in return. It does feel good to help someone.

"Kenzie, it's your turn," José says. "Why don't you take a run down the hill?"

I strap on my board. Everyone is watching me. I realize that they expect me to be grumpy like usual.

It's time to show them what I can do. It's time to show them what happens when you take a chance.

I zoom down the hill, carving curves and gaining speed until I've left everyone behind in the dust . . . er, the snow.

GLOSSARY

avalanche (AV-uh-lanch)—a large mass of snow, ice, or earth that suddenly moves down the side of a mountain

awkward (AWK-wurd)—difficult or embarrassing

especially (ess-PESH-uh-lee)—more than usually; particularly

gliding (GLIDE-ing)—moving smoothly and easily

horizontal (hor-uh-ZON-tuhl)—flat and parallel to the ground

misadventures (miss-ad-VEN-churs)—accidents

rail (rayl)—in snowboarding, a fixed metal bar that riders slide across as a trick

shrugs (SHRUHGS)—raises shoulders in order to show doubt or lack of interest

wobble (WOB-uhl)—to move unsteadily from side to side

ABOUT THE AUTHOR

JESSICA GUNDERSON

Jessica Gunderson grew up in the prairies of North Dakota, where there was a lot of snow but no mountains, so she never tried snowboarding. But her husband, Jason, loves to snowboard. She thinks she may try it someday, and hopefully she'll love it just as much as Kenzie does. She currently lives in Madison, Wisconsin, with her husband and a large white cat who looks like a snowy mountain.

ABOUT THE ILLUSTRATOR

JORGE SANTILLAN

Jorge Santillan got his start illustrating in the children's sections of local newspapers. He opened his own illustration studio in 2005. His creative team specializes in books, comics, and children's magazines. Jorge lives in Mendoza, Argentina, with his wife, Bety; son, Luca; and their four dogs, Fito, Caro, Angie, and Sammy.

SNOWBOARDING IN HISTORY

1929 M.J. "Jack" Burchett secures a plywood plank to his feet and rides down a snowy hill. This is the first known "snowboard."

1965 Sherman Poppen connects two skis and attaches a rope to the front. He calls it the **snurfer**.

1977 Jake Burton begins Burton Snowboards. He is the first person to put foot bindings on the board.

1979 Paul Graves introduces snurfer tricks including flips, 360 spins, and grabs.

1981 Ski areas begin **banning** snowboarding because skiers do not like it.

1989 Five large, popular ski resorts allow snowboarding.

1997 Snowboarders compete in the first winter **X-games**.

1998 Snowboarding becomes an Olympic sport.

2006 Americans **Hannah Teter** and Shaun White win gold in their halfpipe snowboard events at the Winter Olympics.

2010 Knowing he has won the gold medal, **Shaun White** thrills Olympic crowds by performing his famous trick, the Double McTwist.

FIG. 1

FIG. 2

Kenzie Winz
Comes Out on Top!

If you liked Kenzie's snowboarding adventure, check out her other sports stories.

Don't Break the Balance Beam!

Kenzie's super strength makes her a super tumbler. But when she doesn't control her strength on the beam, it's a disaster. Now all of her teammates are laughing and saying one thing: don't break the balance beam!

There's a Hurricane in the Pool!

Kenzie hates swimming in gym class. She tried to control her strength during her laps, but then she falls behind everyone. When she lets loose, her kicks cause huge waves. Before she knows what's happening, there's a hurricane in the pool!

VICTORY SCHOOL SUPERSTARS

Sports Illustrated KIDS

STONE ARCH BOOKS
a capstone imprint